DISNEP

CINDERELLA

Kindness and Courage

By Rico Green

Based on the Screenplay by Chris Weitz

Executive Producer Tim Lewis

Produced by
Simon Kinberg
Allison Shearmur
David Barron

Directed by Kenneth Branagh

DISNEP PRESS

Los Angeles · New York

Printed in the United States of America   First Paperback Edition, January 2015   10 9 8 7 6 5 4 3 2 1

ISBN 978-1-4847-1112-5

G658-7729-4-14346

Library of Congress Control Number: 2014938283

For more Disney Press fun, visit www.disneybooks.com

For more Cinderella fun, visit www.disney.com/cinderella

This is the story of Ella.

Ever since she was little,
Ella was kind and good.

She cared about animals.

When she found a lost bird,

Ella returned it to its mother.

Ella's father taught her to be good.

Her mother said kindness had power.

Ella promised to be kind.

She promised to have courage.

One sad day, Ella's mother passed away.

Later, Ella's father remarried.

His new wife had two daughters.

Ella faced the change with courage.

She welcomed her new family.

Ella put out food for her mouse
friends.

Her new family had a mean cat.

She wanted the mice to be okay.

Ella's stepfamily was also mean.

They made Ella wait on them.

Ella's father traveled a lot.

It was hard.

But still, Ella tried to be kind.

Then Ella's father passed away.

Ella was very sad.

And her stepfamily grew crueler.

They made her do all the chores.

Ella slept near the fireplace.

So they called her Cinderella.

One day, Ella rode through the forest.

She wanted to clear her head.

Ella saw some men hunting.

She bravely saved a stag from the hunt.

Then Ella met a man named Kit.

Kit liked how brave Ella was.

Ella liked how sweet Kit was.

Ella got ready for a royal ball.

She hoped Kit would be there.

But Ella's stepfamily was jealous.

Ella had beauty and grace.

They didn't want her to go to the ball.

So they ripped up her dress.

Ella's stepfamily went to the ball.

Ella stayed home and cried.

Then an old beggar woman came.

She needed help.

Ella gave her food and drink.

But the woman was not a beggar at all.
She turned into Ella's fairy godmother!

She rewarded Ella for her kindness.

She cast a spell.

The Fairy Godmother would help
Ella get to the ball.

She turned a pumpkin into a carriage.

She turned the mice into horses.

The spell also fixed Ella's dress.

It gave her glass slippers.

Ella looked and felt beautiful.

She would go to the royal ball

after all!

It was a dream come true.

Ella climbed into the magic carriage.

She made her way to the ball.

She couldn't wait to have a nice night.

And she couldn't wait to see Kit.

Ella knew everything would be okay.

She had kindness and courage.

She had power and magic on her side.

And she would live *happily ever after.*